The Sloth Life

Dream On!

FROM FLYING TO FALLING: WHAT YOUR DREAMS REVEAL ABOUT YOU.

TO MY BROTHER WARD. —K.M.

Art copyright © 2020 by Kyla May Dinsmore
Text copyright © 2020 by Scholastic Inc.

All rights reserved. Published by Scholastic Inc., *Publishers since 1920.* SCHOLASTIC and associated logos are trademarks and/or registered trademarks of Scholastic Inc.

The publisher does not have any control over and does not assume any responsibility for author or third-party websites or their content.

No part of this publication may be reproduced, stored in a retrieval system, or transmitted in any form or by any means, electronic, mechanical, photocopying, recording, or otherwise, without written permission of the publisher. For information regarding permission, write to Scholastic Inc., Attention: Permissions Department, 557 Broadway, New York, NY 10012.

ISBN 978-1-338-66622-9

10 9 8 7 6 5 4 3 2 1   20 21 22 23 24

Printed in the U.S.A.   40
First printing 2020

Book design by Jessica Meltzer

The Sloth Life

Dream On!

FROM FLYING TO FALLING: WHAT YOUR DREAMS REVEAL ABOUT YOU.

By JOAN EMERSON

ILLUSTRATED BY kylamay

SCHOLASTIC INC.

TABLE OF CONTENTS

THIS IS SLOTH.

I LIKE TO PARTY
AND BY PARTY
I MEAN TAKE NAPS

SLOTH
AROUND TOWN

AT THE MOVIES

AT THE LIBRARY

AT THE PLAYGROUND

AT THE BUS STOP

ON THE BUS

AT THE COFFEE SHOP

AT THE POOL

SHOPPING LIST

- ☑ Sleepytime tea
- ☑ Napkins
- ☑ Ice dream

AT THE PARK

AT THE DOG PARK

AT THE
TRAMPOLINE PARK

AT THE HAIRDRESSER

AT THE NAIL SALON

AT THE MALL

SLIPPERS R US

SLIPPERS R US

SLIPPERS R US

AT THE FIRE STATION

AT THE POLICE STATION

IN A TAXI CAB

IN HIS HAPPY PLACE

SLOTH
THROUGHOUT
THE YEAR

WINTER

SPRING

SUMMER

FALL

SPRING BREAK

WINTER BREAK

FALL FIELD TRIP

WELCOME TO
SLEEPY HOLLOW,
HOME OF
THE INFAMOUS
HEA...

HOW TO IMPROVE YOURSELF THIS YEAR

SET DAILY GOALS

TODAY'S GOALS:

- ☑ Sleep
- ☑ Nap
- ☑ Relax
- ☐ Exercise?

WORKOUT
WITH A FRIEND

SAY "NO" TO MORE THINGS

MAKE TIME FOR YOURSELF

BE FLEXIBLE WITH YOUR SCHEDULE

TODAY'S SCHEDULE:

Breakfast 9am

Nap ~~11am-1pm~~ 10am-5pm

Dinner 6pm

Bedtime 9pm

LEARN A NEW SKILL

START A DAILY MEDITATION PRACTICE

SIGN UP FOR AN EXTRACURRICULAR ACTIVITY

SEEK OUT A ROLE MODEL

MEET AND
GREET WITH
RIP VAN WINKLE,
THE MAN
WHO SLEPT
FOR 20 YEARS!

SEARCH FOR DEEPER MEANING

TAKE MORE NAPS

HOLIDAYS WITH
SLOTH

NEW YEAR'S EVE

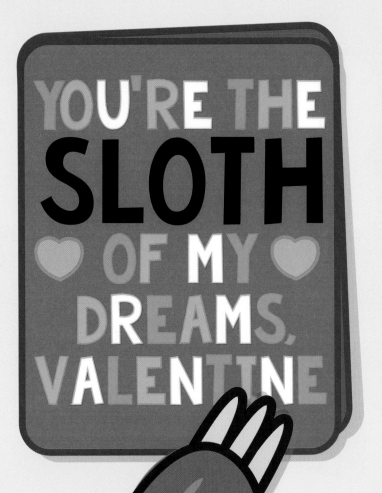

44

TUNNEL OF NAPS

ST. PATRICK'S DAY

EASTER

4TH OF JULY

"Oh beautiful
for spacious beds,
for the amber
nightlight glow . . ."

HALLOWEEN

A HISTORY OF SLOTH'S
COSTUME CONTEST
WINS AND LOSSES

PARTICIPATION
AWARD

A GHOST

3RD PLACE

SLEEPING BEAUTY

2ND PLACE

COUCH POTATO

SLEEPERMAN

GRAND
CHAMPION

SLOTHSGIVING

I AM THANKFUL FOR:

Fluffy slippers

Polkadot PJs

Night lights

Fuzzy blankets

Broken alarm clocks

Snow days

HANUKKAH

SLOTH'S
GUIDE TO TRAVEL

DAY ONE:

ENJOY A MOVIE ON YOUR FLIGHT

DAY TWO:
DO SOME SIGHTSEEING

DAY THREE:
SEE A SHOW

DAY FOUR:

GET SOME TIPS FROM THE LOCALS

SEARCH

best places to nap
in New York City

DAY FIVE:
PRETEND YOU'RE A LOCAL

CENTRAL PARK

DAY SIX:
REST

DAY SEVEN:

CATCH SOME SHUT-EYE ON YOUR RETURN FLIGHT

DAY EIGHT:
RECOVER

HAPPY BIRTHDAY, SLOTH!

You're invited to . . .

A SLUMBER PARTY*

for Sloth's Birthday!

DRESS TO IMPRESS
Silliest pajamas win a prize!

B.Y.O.P.
(Bring Your Own Pillow)

*To be clear:
We will actually slumber. This is not
a stay-up-all-night thing. If you thought
that, do you even know me at all?!

—Sloth

SLOTH'S GIFT GUIDE

ACCEPTABLE:
CACTUS NIGHT-LIGHT

UNACCEPTABLE:
CACTUS PILLOW

ACCEPTABLE: CHIC SLEEP MASK

UNACCEPTABLE: CREEPY HORROR MASK

ACCEPTABLE:
COZY PJs

UNACCEPTABLE:
LIGHT-UP PJs

ACCEPTABLE: ELECTRIC BLANKET

UNACCEPTABLE: ELECTRIC GUITAR

SLOTH
SLEEPING
POSITIONS:
A SAMPLING

THE SNOW ANGEL

THE OPERA SINGER

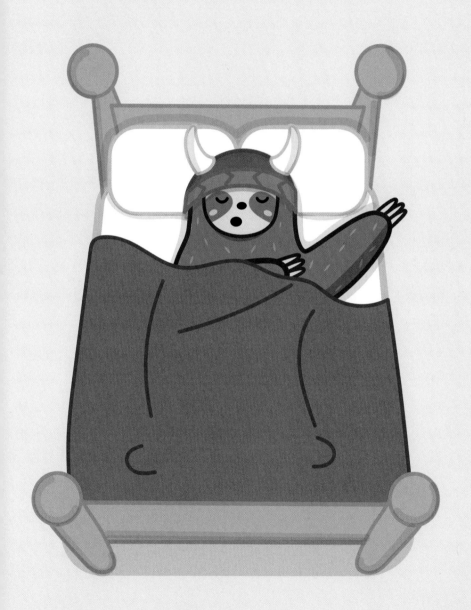

THE GYMNAST

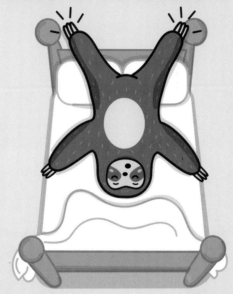

THE CANNONBALLER

THE SWAN LAKER

THE SWORD FIGHTER

THE DISCO DANCER

THE Y.M.C.A.

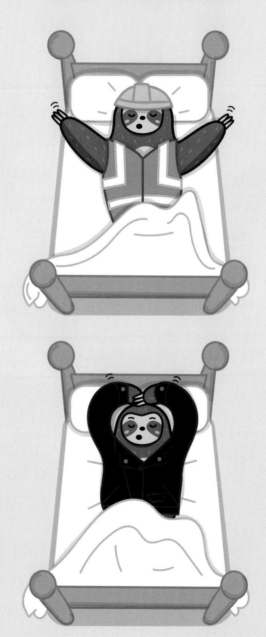

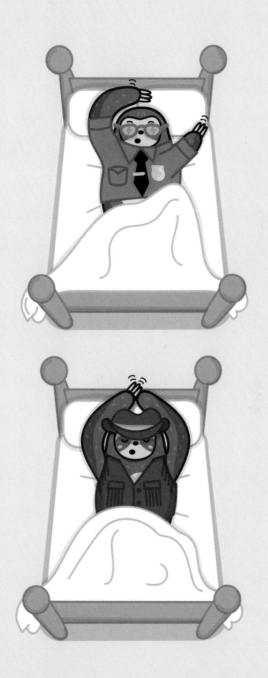

THINGS TO DO
ON YOUR
DAY OFF

WATCH THE CLOUDS GO BY

READ THOSE BOOKS YOU'VE BEEN MEANING TO READ

The Chronicles of Yawn-ia

Alice's Adventures in Slumberland

The Wind in the Pillows

Winnie the Snooze

A Wrinkle in Bedtime

The Adventures of Snuggleberry Sloth

James and the Giant Nap

TRY A NEW EXERCISE CLASS

EARN SOME EXTRA CASH

EARN EVEN MORE EXTRA CASH

GO TO A CONCERT

GO TO A GAME

GO MATTRESS
SHOPPING

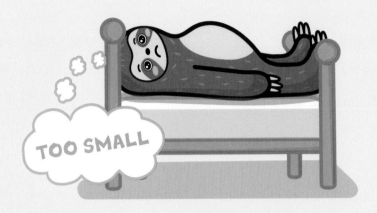

103

START A
NEW PROJECT

IDEAS FOR
SLOTH'S VLOG:

1. Pajama haul
2. Comfiest pillow review
3. Under eye make-up tricks
4. A how-to on sleeping wherever, whenever

BECOME INTERNET FAMOUS

EVERYONE
DESERVES TO BE COZY!

Contribute to our
BLANKET DRIVE
today!

REARRANGE YOUR PILLOW COLLECTION

REARRANGE YOUR STUFFIE COLLECTION

DREAM ON